Little, Whale's Song

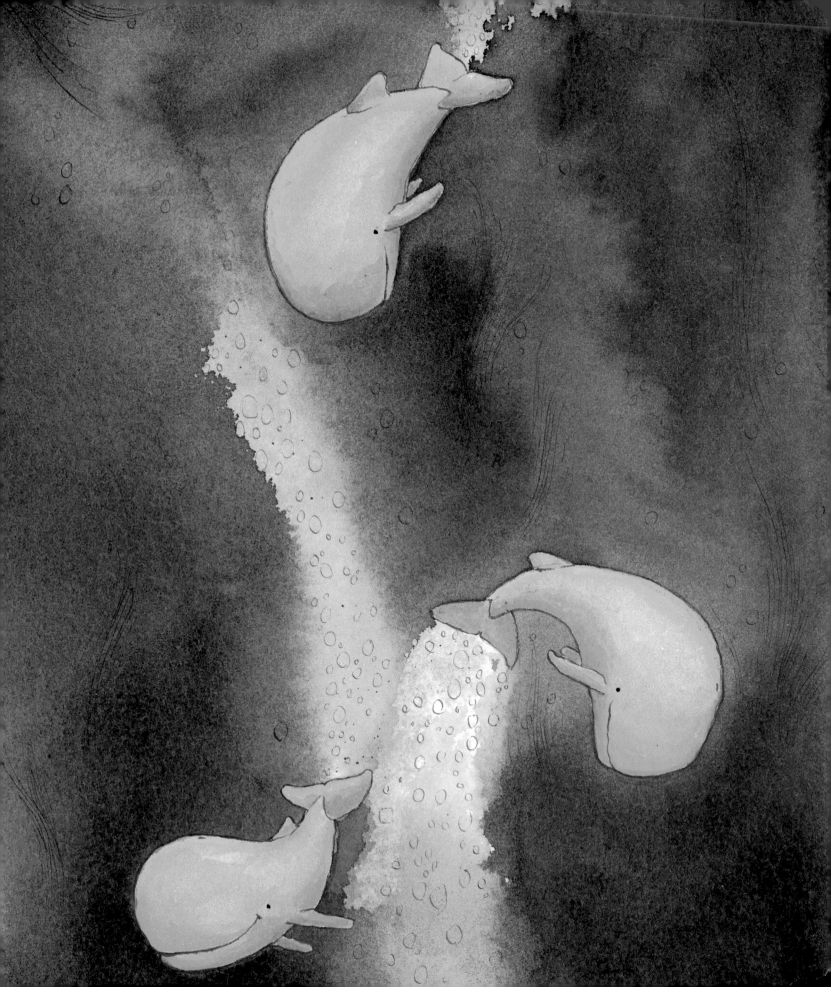

To Sal and Matt and Chris

Published by Hinkler Books Pty Ltd
45–55 Fairchild Street
Heatherton Victoria 3202 Australia
www.hinkler.com.au

hinkler

First published by Piccadilly Press Ltd., London

Text © Fran Evans 2003
Illustrations © Fran Evans 2003
Cover design © Hinkler Books 2011

Cover design: Peter Tovey and Mandi Cole
Prepress: Graphic Print Group

ISBN: 978 1 7435 2449 7

Printed and bound in China

Little Whale's Song

Fran Evans

hinkler

Little Whale was busy playing with the fish on the ocean floor. So he didn't see his family swimming away without him.

Little Whale was frightened.
He tried to make a singing-call to his family,
but no sound came out.

Somehow he'd forgotten how to sing.
He felt so lonely and sad.

Little Whale noticed a dolphin just above
him. "Can you help me to sing?
What sound do you make?"
"*Squeak, squeak, click, click, squeak,*" said the
dolphin.

But Little Whale couldn't squeak or click,
so he swam away.

Then Little Whale came across a lobster.
"Can you help me to sing? What sound do
you make?" Little Whale asked.

"*Bzz, bzz, bzzz*," hummed the lobster,
like a honeybee.
But Little Whale couldn't work out how
to hum.

An octopus floated by, and Little Whale called out, "Can you help me to sing?"
But the octopus just changed colour and danced away, moving all his eight tentacles.

Then Little Whale saw a turtle.
He hurried towards it.
"I've forgotten how to sing," said Little Whale.

But the turtle tucked itself into its shell and floated away.
"Wait!" called Little Whale, following it up and up.

Suddenly Little Whale reached the surface.
A seal was sunning herself on a rock.
"Oh, please," said Little Whale, "can *you*
teach me to sing?"

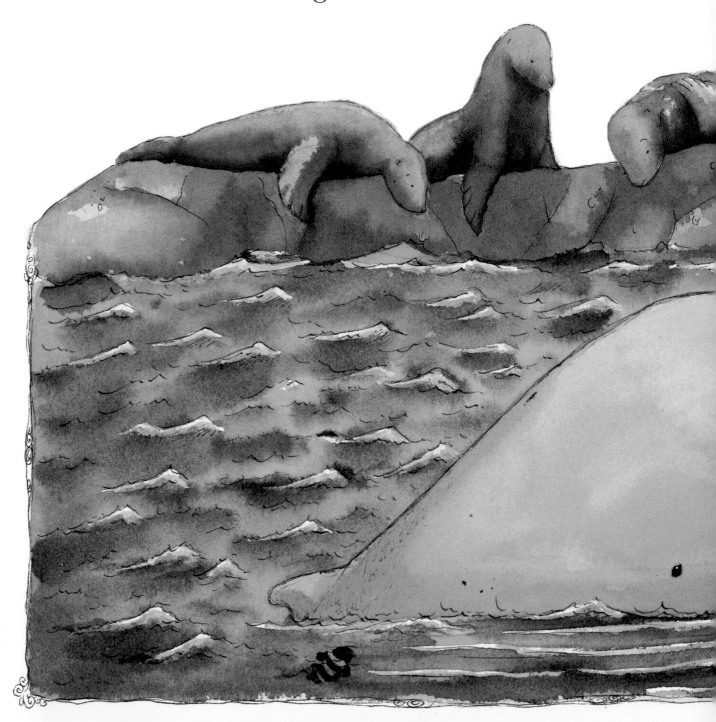

The seal slapped and clapped and honked, but Little Whale couldn't honk – and he didn't want to, either!

Little Whale didn't know what to do.
He flicked his tail.
He shot straight up out of the water.

And he took a deep breath and sprayed
water out of his blowhole.

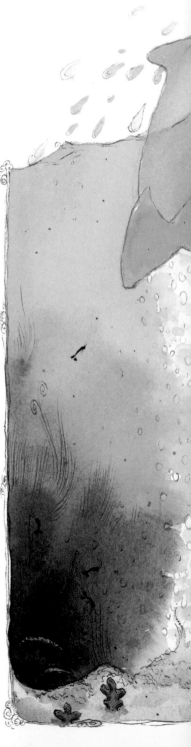

But still he couldn't sing.

Little Whale felt sorry for himself. "I've asked *everyone*," he whimpered, "and I still can't sing."

Then a wise Manatee swam over to him. "No one else can teach you your sound – you must listen to your *own* voice. Why don't you try and make a sound all of your own?"

Sad Little Whale let out a huge, loud, moany sigh. And . . .

. . . he sighed again. It was a *big* sound.

He sighed again . . . a happy sing-song sigh . . .

Suddenly Little Whale was singing his
family call-song!

And he heard a faint sound in the distance.

It was his family answering him. They were coming back to find him.

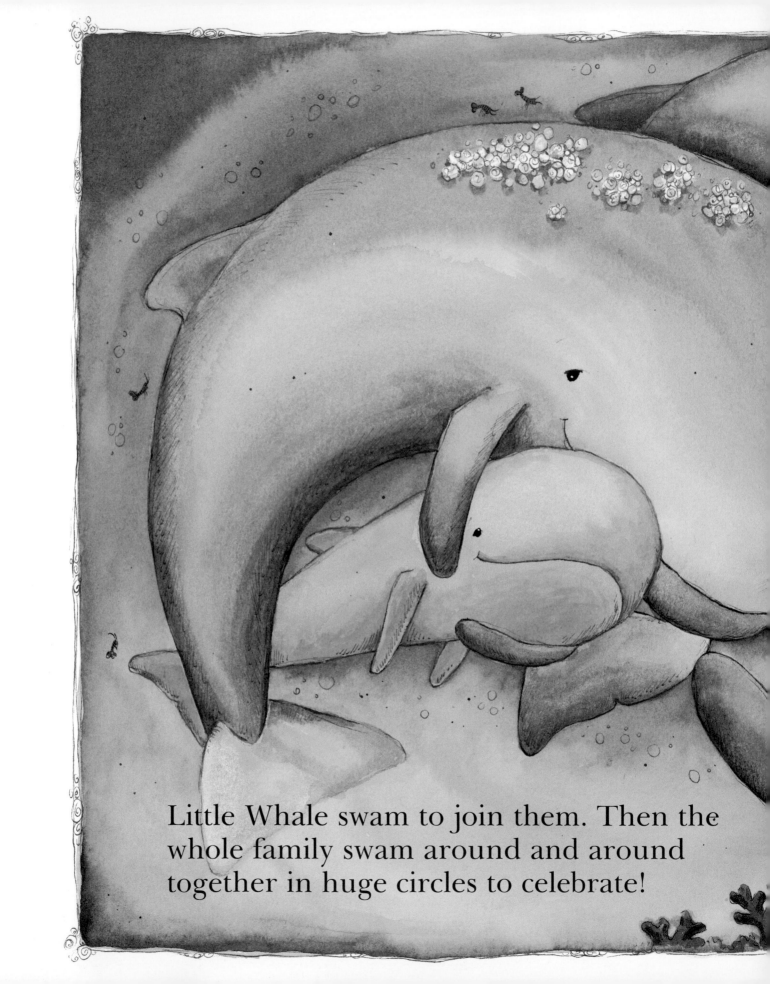

Little Whale swam to join them. Then the whole family swam around and around together in huge circles to celebrate!

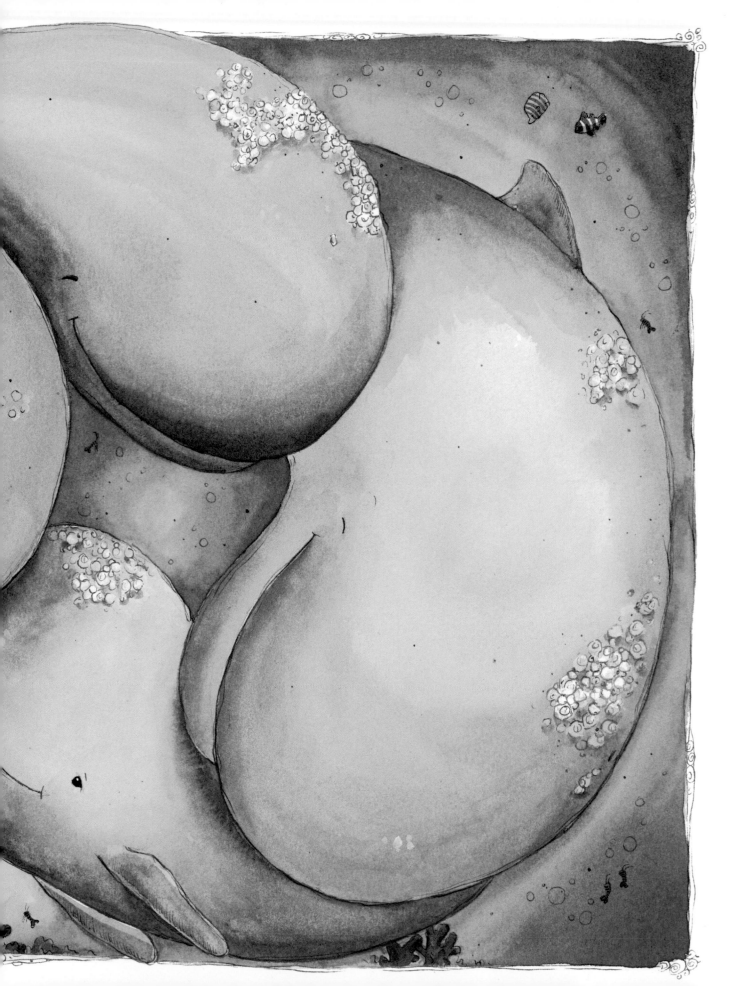

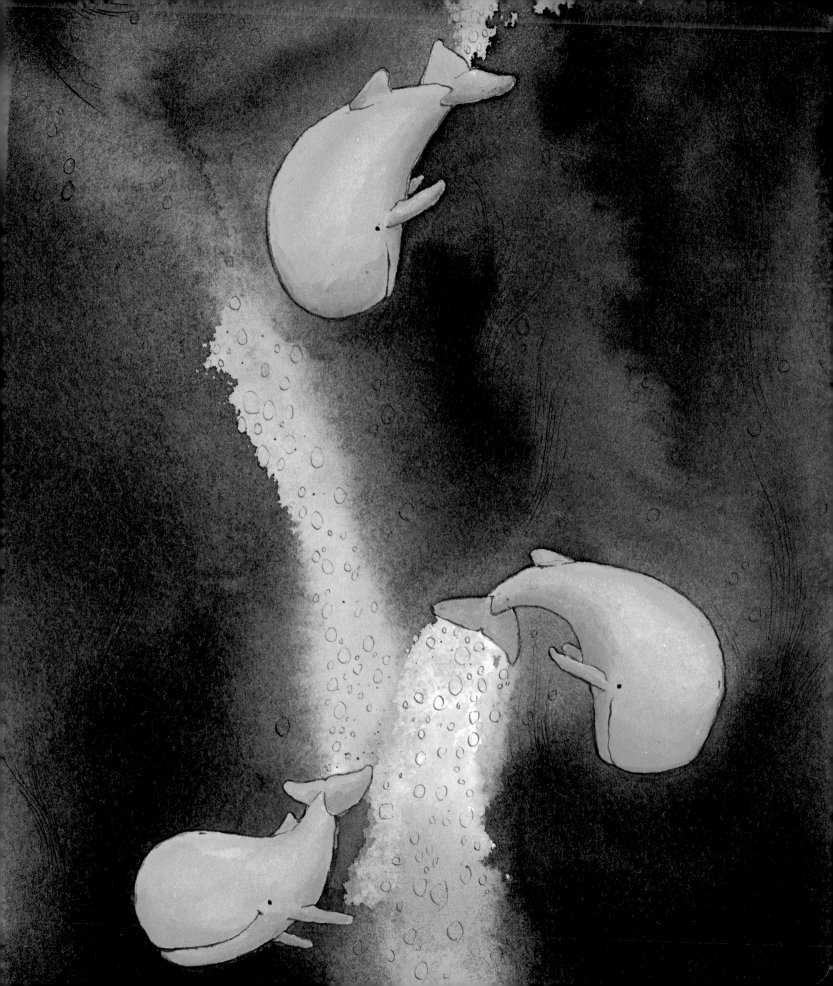